BEANO®
THE DAY THE TEACHERS
DISAPPEARED

Craig Graham & Mike Stirling

Illustrated by Vivian Truong

Farshore

First published in Great Britain 2024 by Farshore
An imprint of HarperCollins*Publishers*
1 London Bridge Street, London, SE1 9GF
www.farshore.co.uk

HarperCollins*Publishers*
Macken House, 39/40 Mayor Street Upper,
Dublin 1, D01 C9W8, Ireland

Written by Craig Graham & Mike Stirling
Illustrated by Vivian Truong
Additional Illustration – Ed Stockham
Creative Services Manager – Rhiannon Tate
Executive Producer – Rob Glenny
Text design by Janene Spencer

BEANO

BEANO.COM

A Beano Studios Product © DC Thomson Ltd (2024)

ISBN 978 0 00 861528 4
Printed in Great Britain
003

Stay safe online. Any website addresses listed in this book are correct at the
time of going to print. However, Farshore is not responsible for content hosted
by third parties. Please be aware that online content can be subject to change
and websites can contain content that is unsuitable for children. We advise
that all children are supervised when using the internet.

★ **The star of this book is:** ★

_____

Dear [insert new pupil's name here],

As you will be joining us here at Bash Street School next term, I thought I would write to you to pass on some important information for when you start.

You will be in Class 3C, and your teacher will be Miss Mistry. She is very nice, and you will like her very much, I'm sure - even if she does have very modern ideas about children and teaching.

There are toilets on every floor of the school, but I prefer the ones on floor 2. They smell much nicer.

A school uniform can be purchased at Madame Bovary's No-Frills Clothing Emporium, which is on Yawn Street, right next to Sheena's Sensible Shoes, which I also recommend.

On your first day, please report to the school office, where Mrs Yodel will register you and give you directions to Class 3C.

Yours educationally,

Mrs E. Creecher

Dear Bash Street Kid!

How exciting that you will be joining us at Bash Street School next term!

Your class is 3C and it's the best class in the whole school . . . although I may be biased as it is also MY class! I'm sure you will make lots of very good friends.

When you get to school, ask Mrs Yodel at the office to give me a call and I will come to collect you and bring you to class.

I will pick someone from the class (they're all lovely) to be your Bash Street Buddy, and it will be their special privilege to make sure you can find your way around the school.

See you soon!

Miss Mistry :)

PS – I've attached a picture of the school with a few notes from your classmates, which will help you get to know your way around.

Bash Street School for Beginners!

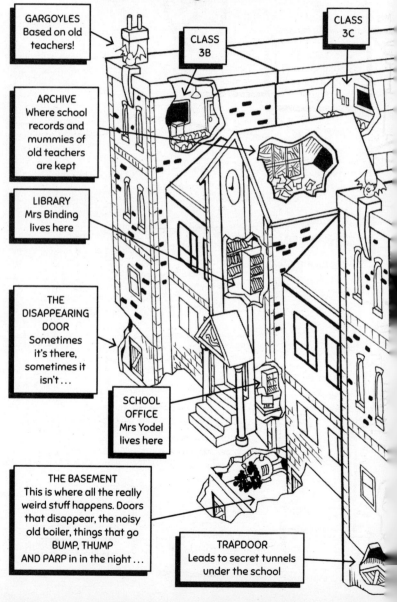

GARGOYLES
Based on old teachers!

CLASS 3B

CLASS 3C

ARCHIVE
Where school records and mummies of old teachers are kept

LIBRARY
Mrs Binding lives here

THE DISAPPEARING DOOR
Sometimes it's there, sometimes it isn't ...

SCHOOL OFFICE
Mrs Yodel lives here

THE BASEMENT
This is where all the really weird stuff happens. Doors that disappear, the noisy old boiler, things that go BUMP, THUMP AND PARP in in the night ...

TRAPDOOR
Leads to secret tunnels under the school

All you need to know about the best school in Beanotown, by Class 3C!

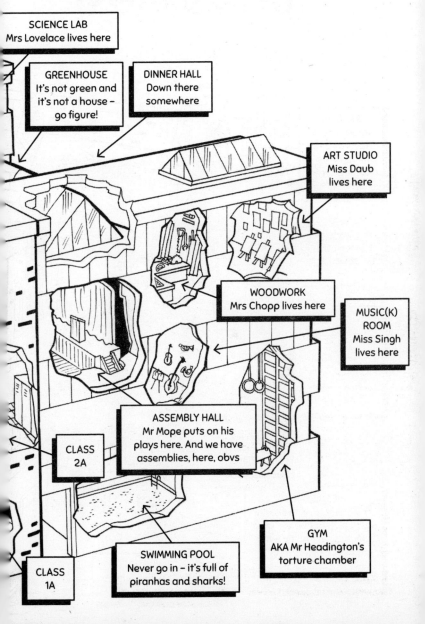

SCIENCE LAB
Mrs Lovelace lives here

GREENHOUSE
It's not green and
it's not a house –
go figure!

DINNER HALL
Down there
somewhere

ART STUDIO
Miss Daub
lives here

WOODWORK
Mrs Chopp lives here

MUSIC(K)
ROOM
Miss Singh
lives here

ASSEMBLY HALL
Mr Mope puts on his
plays here. And we have
assemblies, here, obvs

CLASS
2A

CLASS
1A

SWIMMING POOL
Never go in – it's full of
piranhas and sharks!

GYM
AKA Mr Headington's
torture chamber

HOW TO READ THIS BOOK!

This book will make NO SENSE if you read it from front to back like a normal book!

That's because YOU choose what happens and how the story ends!

Don't worry – it's easy. Every few pages, you'll be given a choice, like this:

If you want to fart like an elephant, go to page 93

If you want to burp like a Brontosaurus, go to page 875

All you have to do is decide which option you'd rather do, and follow the instructions!

Got it? Great! You're ready to begin!

GO TO THE NEXT PAGE!

GOOD MORNING, BEANOTOOOOOWN!

The birds wake you up early, but you aren't tired. You're excited!

Today is your first day at a new school, and not just any old school, either! Today, you are going to join Class 3C at Bash Street School.

And that means **YOU** are about to become a **BASH STREET KID!** You're new to town, but you already know that the Bash Street Kids are the coolest, smartest, funniest kids around. And you can't wait to be one of them.

You and your family only moved to Beanotown on Saturday. Today is Monday, so you've only been here for two days, but you already like it here. It seems just like the place you used to call home, only everything here is . . . funnier!

For instance, you know those birds that woke you up? They aren't just twittering, chirping and tweeting like the birds that used to sound your alarm. They're singing Swift's greatest hits (no, not *that* Swift)!

You jump out of bed and throw on your new school uniform: a greyish blue sweater over a white shirt with a skinny black and white striped tie. You're not sure you like it, but no one ever likes their school uniform, do they?

After breakfast, you grab your stuff, shout 'goodbye' and step out into the warm Beanotown sunshine.

58 Gasworks Road, Beanotown, you think. *What a cool new home address!*

You walk down the path and out of the gate onto Gasworks Road.

As you walk past number 51, a spiky-haired boy wearing a red-and-black striped jumper emerges from the front door, followed by a little black dog with enormous teeth. Number 51 looks like it's had quite a hard life, and the garage door is held shut by a plank of wood nailed right across it. The boy stops when he sees you.

'Hi!' he says. 'You're the new kid from number 58, aren't you?'

You nod and tell him your name.

'I'm in class 3C,' you tell him.

'Me too!' says Dennis. 'We can be friends!'

'Really? But where's your uniform?'

'Bash Street School doesn't have a uniform,' says Dennis. 'Well, it does, but you don't have to wear it unless you want to. And I don't want to!'

You do a quick calculation in your head and realise that you don't have time to run back into the house to change into your favourite outfit. School uniform it is!

You give Gnasher a pat, nervously at first, but he seems to like it. You pretend not to notice the fleas doing the conga along his spine.

CHEW, CHEW, CHEW, COME ON AND DO THE CONGA...

'I know a top-secret, super-cool shortcut to school,' says Dennis. 'I can show you if you like?'

If you want to see Dennis's cool shortcut, go to page 7

If you think the shortcut sounds too risky, go to page 13

DENNIS AND GNASHER'S SHORTCUT!

'I love shortcuts!' you say.

'Come on then,' says Dennis, walking in the **WRONG** direction . . . *away* from where you thought the school was.

'Are you sure this is the right way?' you ask, catching up.

'In my experience,' says Dennis. 'You don't have to worry about finding school. It will find *you*, no matter how hard you try to avoid it.'

Dennis's 'shortcut' isn't very short. It takes you half-way up Mount Beano, around the edge of Lake Mess – where you think you spot the Lake Mess Monster (you can't be 100% sure, because what you see looks a lot like a log that just happens to look like a monster) – and then deep into Beanotown Woods.

Suddenly, Dennis stops.

UH-OH!

In front of you is a muddy stream, which you just *know* is too wide to jump over.

'School's that way,' says Dennis, pointing to the far side of the stream.

You look around and spot a rope tied to a tree.

'A rope swing!' you cry, grabbing the rope. Okay, so 'rope' might have been optimistic. It's more of a thick, tatty blue string. Still, it's better than nothing!

Beanotown's like that, you think. *If you find yourself in a spot of bother, there's always a way out of it, if you stay positive and look hard enough.*

You test the rope, then run towards the stream. *Here goes nothing!* At the last moment, you lift your feet, hold on tightly to the rope and sail upwards.

Miraculously, the rope holds and you fly across the stream, letting go and landing in a crouch on the other side.

'Easy!' you say, swinging the rope back to Dennis on the other side.

He ignores it.

'I think I can jump it,' he says, taking five big steps backwards.

'Dennis, no! It's too far!'

Dennis runs towards the stream as fast as

he can, Gnasher racing beside him. You hold your breath – can you even watch? Dennis takes off! His epic leap goes brilliantly until . . .

SPLATTER!

Dennis belly flops into the mud. Gnasher doesn't make it either, landing head-first beside him.

Dennis and his faithful pal drag themselves through the mud towards you, looking like zombies crawling their way out of a graveyard in the middle of a flood.

'I didn't make it,' Dennis says.

'Obvs!' you say. 'And I don't think we're going to make it to school on time, either.'

'Chill,' says Dennis. 'It's right there – look!'

He's right. Bash Street School *is* right there, and – it's a miracle – despite your epic adventures with Dennis, the clock on the front of the school says it's four minutes to nine o'clock.

'Come on!' you cry.

Turn to page 16

12

IT'S TOO EARLY FOR FUN!

'Oh, a shortcut sounds like fun, but I promised I'd stick to the route I already practised. I'll see you in class?'

'That's cool. Maybe tomorrow,' says Dennis. 'See you in 3C!'

He and Gnasher run off.

In *completely* the wrong direction.

You shrug. You like Dennis. He seems like a fun person to know. And Gnasher is awesome!

You walk down Gasworks Road, then turn onto Bash Street. You need to cross the road, so you stand at the kerb and look both ways for traffic.

'Hi there!' calls a familiar voice from behind you.

It's Dennis and Gnasher!

Only now they're sweating, out of breath and covered in mud.

'**GNASH!**' says Gnasher, shaking mud from his fur.

'I thought you knew a shortcut,' you say. 'I got here just as quickly as you.'

Dennis flicks away the mud he just picked out of his ear, like a brown bogey.

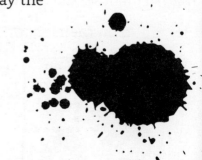

Despite being covered from head to toe in mud, it looks like Dennis and Gnasher had a lot of fun on their 'shortcut'. Maybe you'll go with them next time.

Go to page 16

ARE YOU TOO COOL FOR BASH STREET SCHOOL?

To get into Bash Street School, you walk
through two impressive iron gates, with not one
but *two* headteachers staring sternly at you.

They can't help staring – they're statues and everyone knows that statues don't blink. Not when you're looking at them, at least.

You really should be more nervous, but the gates are held on with sticky tape and one of the statues has a traffic cone on its head. It's more silly than scary.

'The pupils' door is round the back,' says Dennis. 'The office is just inside the front door.'

'Thanks,' you say. 'See you in a bit!'

Dennis and Gnasher sprint round the corner and out of sight. You open the front door and step into the school hallway.

You've never seen so many gigantic houseplants in your life! It's like a jungle in there. You find your way through to the office and look for someone to speak to – a name plate on the desk tells you that it should be a Mrs Yodel – but there's no one there.

The school bell rings and the corridor fills with noisy pupils making their way to class. The stampede dwindles to a trickle, then the school is quiet again, with just the occasional sprinting, red-faced latecomer disturbing the peace.

It's five minutes past nine and there's still no Mrs Yodel.

You decide to wait in case she's just gone for a tinkle.

At 9:10 you decide to wait just a little longer in case Mrs Yodel has gone for a poo.

At 9:15 you decide Mrs Yodel must be

having a really bad toilet morning, and you'd rather come back later.

It's time to meet your new classmates!

There are signs on the wall that show you the way to Class 3C. Up two flights of stairs, then turn right. Turn right again and the class door is along the corridor, on the left.

As you get closer, you can hear chatting and laughter from inside. You take a deep breath and walk in.

SILENCE! Thirteen sets of eyes blink at you.

'Well, what have we here?' says a tall boy sitting on a desk at the front of the class.

DOES BASH STREET SCHOOL HAVE A NEW PUPIL?

19

The boy is very smartly dressed in the same uniform as you, but fancier somehow. He's swapped the official black and white skinny tie for a fancy pink, silk version. It yells out **POSH!** An expensive-looking briefcase sits open on the desk in front of him with neat rows of fancy fountain pens strapped inside.

'I'm Walter Brown,' the boy drawls. 'My dad is the mayor of Beanotown.'

'Hello,' you say, and introduce yourself.

You notice Dennis waving at you from the back of the class.

'HEY!' he shouts. 'I saved you a seat!'

'You can sit here,' says Walter, pushing a smartly dressed boy off the seat beside him. 'There's a vacancy in the Circle of Power, and you're dressed for the part.'

'What's the Circle of Power?' you ask.

'That's what I call my very best friends,' says Walter. 'I'm at the centre of the circle and they surround me with complete loyalty.'

'Why is there a vacancy?' you ask, eyeing the boy picking himself off the floor and scampering off to another desk.

'Simon forgot to bring my packed lunch today,' says Walter, turning to glare at the boy now sitting down a couple of rows behind them. 'That's where he used to sit. Now he's outside the Circle of Power until he redeems himself. You're uninvited to my pool party this weekend!' he shouts.

'Pool party?' you ask.

'Walter has the best pool in Beanotown at his house,' says the boy sat behind him, who looks like he slept in his uniform.

'Yes, Bertie's right. You don't want to go to Beanotown's public pool. *Someone's* little sister,' he threw a disgusted look in Dennis's direction, 'once had a massive poo in it. Only members of the Circle of Power are allowed to swim in my pool.'

'I see,' you say.

'So, do you want to be a member?' Walter asks, offering you the seat beside him.

If you decide to sit with Walter, go to page 24

If you decide to sit with Dennis, go to page 55

WALTER WAY TO MAKE FRIENDS!

You sit down.

'So, who else is in the Circle of Power?' you ask cheerfully.

'Bertie, Dudley and Susan,' says Walter, waving his arm towards the other kids wearing the school uniform, sitting at the desks around him.

Bertie is smiling at you, which is more than you can say for Dudley, who has his tie done up so tightly that his collar is cutting into his neck, or Susan who looks like she's sucking on a particularly sour sweet.

'Just the three of you? That's more like a Triangle of Power,' you joke. No one laughs.

You sit in silence for a couple of minutes. Meanwhile, Walter is fiddling with something in his briefcase.

'Did you do anything nice at the weekend?' you ask Bertie. He looks like the friendliest of your new chums.

'We went to watch the horse races,' he replies. 'Father had a runner in the 3:15 at . . .'

'**SHH!**' hisses Susan. 'The first rule of the Circle of Power is that we only speak when Walter speaks!'

'What's the second rule?' you ask. 'We only fart when Walter farts?'

Susan looks horrified.

WALTER NEVER FARTS!

Walter shuts his briefcase with a snap.

'That's right!' he says. 'We leave childish things like that to the dreadful people sat over there.'

Walter is furious.

Dudley fumes.

Susan shakes her fist at them.

Bertie . . . farts. ACTUALLY farts.

Walter is astonished, horrified and absolutely disgusted.

'Sorry, Walter,' says Bertie. 'I was trying to be angry and it just sort of squeaked out!'

You stifle a snort of laughter, trying to turn it into a cough.

'Are you OK?' asks Walter haughtily.

You shake your head. It's no good, you can't hold the laughter in any longer!

Walter stiffens. 'We do not laugh at bottom expulsions in the Circle of Power!'

Go to page 29

AREN'T THERE ANY TEACHERS IN THIS SCHOOL?

It's a struggle, and you feel a bit sweaty, but you manage to stop your laughter before it erupts out through your nose in a loud snort.

'Of course, Walter. You're right,' you say. 'Bottom expulsions are totally disgusting. I won't laugh at them again.'

You wink at Bertie, who grins back at you.

'Have you got a school house yet?' asks Walter, changing subjects.

'I don't think so,' you confess.

Walter smiles, not entirely kindly.

'At this school, there are three houses,' he pronounces. 'Bagge-Shott, Fungus and Sutherland. I am in Bagge-Shott, Bertie is in Fungus and Dudley is in Sutherland.'

'Fungus sounds like fun—' you begin, but Walter interrupts.

'You can join Bagge-Shott,' he says. 'We haven't won the House Trophy in five years, so we could do with some new blood.'

'OK, whatever,' you say, distracted by some excitement at the back of the class.

'What's going on?' muses Walter. 'Dudley, go and find out what the oiks are up to.'

Dudley performs a remarkable feat. He slithers – like a snake – down from his seat to the floor, then silently worms his way between the legs of the desks and chairs until he's close to where Dennis and his friends are chatting excitedly.

Suddenly, a red-haired girl in a jumper that looks quite like but not identical to Dennis's stands up and shouts, very loudly: 'ALL THE

TEACHERS ARE MISSING – THE PUPILS ARE IN CHARGE OF BASH STREET SCHOOL!'

Dudley slithers back to the front of the class. You try not to shudder, but it's seriously creepy.

'It sssssseemssss . . . ' begins Dudley. 'Sorry, I don't know why I do that ssssssometimessss . . . it seems like something has happened to the school staff. None of them can be found anywhere, and Dennis and his friends seem to think they're in charge of the school now . . .'

'Yes, yes!' cries Walter. 'We heard all that when Minnie yelled it out loud. But surely they must know that only I have the leadership qualities to take over this desperate school! Why, when I think of all the amazing changes I would make . . .'

'I'd put a games console on the back of every toilet door,' says Bertie, then, when everyone stares at him, adds: 'I spend a lot of time on the toilet. It gets boring.'

'I would like a separate playground for pupils who would like to play nice games at break,' says Susan.

'I would like a school snake,' says Dudley, licking his lips. 'A python or a boa constrictor maybe.'

AND WHAT'S YOUR FAVOURITE SCHOOL SUBJECT?

HISSSSTORY!

'I'd make all the teachers wear red noses, like clowns,' you say. 'That would be funny!'

'Yes, yes,' says Walter, jabbing away at his phone screen. 'You lot just amuse yourselves with your silly, childish ideas. I've had the best idea of anyone, ever.'

You know whoever Walter is calling picks up, because you can hear them shouting.

'Sorry, Father,' says Walter, flushing pink. 'I-I need to ask your advice . . .'

And with that, Walter leaves the classroom, phone clamped to his ear.

'What's he up to?' you ask the Circle of Power, frowning.

'He'll tell us when he gets back,' says Bertie. 'But he must think it's a good idea if he's called the mayor.'

34

There's more laughter from the back of the room. You look at the Circle of Power, who are watching the door of the class for Walter's return, and sigh.

'I might go over and say hello to Dennis and his friends,' you say. 'I'll be back in a minute.'

'Walter won't like that,' says Dudley. 'That's fraternising with the enemy.'

'Who's going to tell him?' you shoot back.

To leave the Circle of Power and say hello to Dennis and his friends, go to page 76

To stick with the Circle of Power – after all, you love pool parties, go to page 36

THE BEST LAID PLANS OF WALTER BROWN . . .

You don't have to wait long for Walter to come back. He looks very pleased with himself.

'Gather round, everyone,' he says. 'Huddle of Power.'

In the Huddle of Power, Walter tells you all about his plan.

'We're going to dig up the playground and frack for oil and gas,' he whispers.

'What's fracking?' asks Bertie.

You know what fracking is. You did a project about it at your old school.

'It's when you pump water into the ground at a really high pressure,' you explain. 'The idea is that the water forces oil or gas up to the surface, so you can use it as fuel.'

WATER
OIL
DOG
HOLES

'Exactly,' chuckles Walter. 'Only we aren't going to use it ourselves. We're going to sell it back to the school for energy!'

'But you can't!' you exclaim. 'The school needs its playground, and the last thing we should be doing is burning more fossil fuels!'

'Nonsense!' says Walter, although he looks doubtful. 'Anyway, I've already told my dad. The fracking company is on its way'.

You groan, but Walter ignores you.

'Susan and Dudley,' Walter says, 'you go and tell the other classes they should go home – we don't want any interruptions. Bertie, you take our new friend here and guard the playground. Don't let Dennis or any of his friends anywhere near it. I'll join you once I've been to the bathroom. I often have to go when I get excited.'

And with that, Walter strides away, feeling very pleased with himself.

On the way out of the classroom, you spot Dennis flapping his arms wildly at you.

'You go on without me,' you say to Bertie. 'I need a wee.'

You wait for the others to leave, then sneak back into the classroom and introduce yourself to Dennis's friends.

'Hi, I'm Minnie,' says a red-haired girl wearing a black beret with a red pompom on top, sat beside Dennis. 'I'm what you might call the supreme leader of this class, if not the whole school.'

You balk. Is she another Walter?

'Minnie's my cousin,' grins Dennis. 'She talks a lot of rubbish.'

Minnie sticks her tongue out at him. You relax a bit.

A black-haired girl wearing a green t-shirt with a big picture of the sun on it throws herself into the seat next to where you're standing.

'Can you believe people are still putting paper in the plastic recycling bin?' she says. 'I had to sort it all or none of it would have been recycled properly!

'This is Vito,' chuckles Dennis. 'She's all about saving the planet!'

'I'm Rubi,' says another red-haired girl in a wheelchair with all kinds of high-tech gizmos attached to it.

'Cool tech,' you remark.

'Thanks, I invented it all myself,' Rubi replies.

'Rubi's a genius,' says a tall girl with dreadlocks. 'She can invent anything. I'm Jem, by the way.'

'Not anything,' Rubi says, 'but most things, yes.'

'Awesome,' you say.

'My name's Pie Face,' says a kind-looking boy with glasses and a yellow beanie, stuffing what appears to be a pie containing a full-English breakfast into his mouth.

'The name's Badu. Dan Badu,' says a boy wearing a tuxedo. 'But just call me Dan,' he adds quickly.

'Nice tux,' you say.

'Dan's a spy,' says Pie Face, between large bites.

'**SHH!** They're with the enemy!' His eyes narrow on you for a moment.

'I won't tell anyone, promise,' you say, holding up your hands in surrender.

Dan relaxes.

'Speaking of enemies,' Dennis says. 'Am I right in thinking the Circle of Power are up to no good out there?'

You don't say anything.

'We've all got ideas on how we want to make the school a better place for all us kids, and we'd love your help,' says Dennis.

'Dan and I are going to search for the teachers,' says Jem.

'I'm going to up the fun factor of school,' adds Minnie.

'I'm going to bake the biggest pie you've ever seen,' claims Pie Face.

'And I'm going to make the school more energy efficient,' says Rubi.

'Oh! I'll join you for that,' says Vito excitedly.

'You could help me stop whatever evil thing Walter is up to, if you wanted to,' Dennis offers.

> If you're excited and loyal to your new friends in the Circle of Power, go to page 45

> If you decide you can't be a part of Walter's evil scheme, and want to play along as a spy for Dennis and his friends, go to page 168

INSIDE THE CIRCLE OF POWER!

You catch up to Bertie outside, where he's stood scratching his head, watching the workers lug heavy pieces of concrete out of a hole in the centre of the playground.

'Walter wants us to help out,' says Bertie.

'We can't carry that heavy concrete,' you say. 'We'll get hurt!'

'Don't worry,' he says. 'Walter says a lot of things that turn out to be a bad idea. The good thing is that he's just as likely to be mean to you whether you do them or not. Most of the time, I choose not to.'

Three other things Walter has said that turned out to be a BAD IDEA:

- 'monday is Wear A Toga To School Day'
- 'The best place to invest your pocket money is with me!'
- 'Of course no one will notice!'

'Why are you friends with him at all?' you ask. 'You could be friends with any of the kids in Class 3C.'

'The way I see it,' Bertie says, 'is that if Walter wants everybody else to be unhappy then he must be unhappy himself. He's not

so bad, you know. Sure, he's bossy, but he's also generous with his friends. You should see his cinema room! There are definite perks to hanging out with Walter. And if I'm not his friend then who else will do it?'

'Maybe you're right,' you say.

Bertie's mobile phone rings, and he answers it.

'Hi Walter. An elephant? Steal it and get it to help the workers? Er, OK. Bye.'

Bertie hangs up and stuffs his phone into his trouser pocket.

'Walter says Ellis the elephant is out front and we've got to lure him here to help out the workers.'

'An actual elephant?' you ask, filled with wonder at this new school of yours.

'Ellis escapes from the zoo all the time,' explains Bertie. 'Come on, let's go find him.'

When you track down Ellis, he's with three kids you don't recognise: a boy and girl in blue-and-black striped jumpers – the boy patting the elephant and the girl tooting a merry tune . . . with her bottom – and a girl

in a purple hijab sketching out the scene on a tablet.

Ellis is dipping his trunk into a giant bin, then spraying the walls of the school with something sticky, gooey and disgusting. You have no idea why he's doing it, but that's what he's doing.

'That's Sidney, Toots and Sketch Khad –
they're in class 2B,' Bertie explains.

'I've got an idea for how to get Ellis away
from them,' you say. 'But something's bothering
me – is it fair to get him to do all that work?
After all, we can't ask him if he wants to do it.'

'That's what Walter told us to do,' said
Bertie, with a shrug. 'And we can't *make* him
do it if he doesn't want to, can we?'

Bertie's right, you suppose.

You walk over to where Ellis is spraying the
walls with the gloopy muck from the bin.

'That elephant looks thirsty,' you say. 'You
can tell because of all the wrinkles. Elephants
are like peaches – when they dry out, they go
wrinkly like that.'

'Are you sure?' asks Sketch, doubtfully.

'He is pretty wrinkly,' says Toots. 'But I think he always is.'

'I can take him and give him a drink for you, if you like,' you offer.

'That would be great,' says Sidney. You can tell he cares for the elephant a lot. 'Better safe than sorry.'

Bertie grins admiringly at you as you lead Ellis over to the hole the workers are digging. You can't help feeling a bit guilty, though.

'Well done,' he says. 'But can you get him to throw concrete into a dump truck?'

CRUMBS!

You're not so sure. You point at a lump of concrete that a worker is carrying then wave in

the direction of the dump truck.

Ellis nods – well, you *think* he nods – and trots over to the worker.

'Easy,' you say.

'No!' you cry in horror as Ellis throws the worker in instead. 'That's not what I meant!'

WAAAH!

Ellis shoves the dump truck towards the digger, knocking it over like a skittle!

'That wasn't it either!' you cry.

'I don't think this is what Walter had in mind,' says Bertie, cowering. 'At least Ellis is enjoying himself!'

'Wait!' you cry as the workers run away. 'I'll take the elephant back to the zoo!'

But it's no use. They're gone.

'What now?' you ask Bertie.

'I suppose we go back to the class and tell Walter,' he says. 'But it's safe to say we won't be in the Circle of Power anymore!'

Go to page 180

SITTING AT THE BACK IS *SMILES* BETTER!

'I told Dennis I'd sit with him,' you say to Walter. 'Maybe we can chat at break time?'

Walter waves you away like a bad smell.

'Fine,' he says. 'But you'll never be a part of the Circle of Power.'

You make your way to the back of the class.

'What's his problem?' you ask, pointing at Walter.

'Walter? He's always like that,' says Dennis. 'He thinks that because his dad's the mayor, that makes him more important than anybody else. Here, I saved you this seat in front of me.'

'Forget Walter,' interrupts a red-haired girl wearing a black beret with a red pompom on top, sitting beside him. 'I'm Minnie. I'm what you might call the supreme leader of this class, if not the whole school.'

You balk. This isn't another Circle of Power, is it?

MINNIE'S MY COUSIN. SHE TALKS A LOT OF RUBBISH.

Minnie sticks her tongue out at Dennis. You relax a bit.

'I'm Rubi,' says another red-haired girl, sitting in a wheelchair with all kinds of high-tech gizmos attached.

'Cool tech,' you remark.

'Thanks, I invented it all myself,' Rubi replies proudly.

'Rubi's a genius,' says a tall girl with dreadlocks. 'She can invent anything.'

'I'm Jem,' she tells you, fist-bumping with you. 'School wreckathlon champion three years running.'

'Awesome,' you say. 'But don't you mean decathlon champion?'

Jem grins. 'Not at this school!'

'The name's Badu. Dan Badu,' says a boy wearing a tuxedo.

'But just call me Dan,' he adds quickly.

'Nice tux,' you say.

'Dan's a spy,' says a kind-looking boy with glasses and a yellow beanie, stuffing what appears to be a pie containing a full-English breakfast into his mouth.

Dan's eyes narrow on you for a moment.

'I'm a friend, promise,' you say, holding up your hands in surrender.

Dan relaxes.

'My name's Pie Face,' says the boy with the pie.

A black-haired girl wearing a green t-shirt with a big picture of the sun on it throws herself into the seat next to you.

'Can you believe people are still putting paper in the plastic recycling bin?' she says. 'I had to sort it all or none of it would have been recycled properly!'

'This is Vito,' chuckles Dennis. 'She's all about saving the planet!'

You say hi to Vito and tell everyone a bit about yourself.

'What school house are you in?' asks Rubi. You must look a little blank because she carries on, 'Everybody at Bash Street belongs to a school house. There are three: Sutherland, Bagge-Shott and Fungus. '

'You don't get put into a house like at some schools,' says Pie Face. 'You get to choose which one you want to join.'

'And we don't have an evil house or a house that just wins *everything*,' adds Jem.

Minnie goes to the front of the class and returns with a piece of paper.

'This will help you decide which house you want to join,' she says, handing you the paper.

It takes you a while to decide but eventually you tell your new friends which house you want to join.

'Cool!' says Dennis. 'That's decided! I'm in Bagge-Shott and so is Vito. Dan and Minnie are in Fungus together. Jem, Pie Face and Rubi are in Sutherland.'

'What about Gnasher?' you ask.

'He's usually in the doghouse,' laughs Minnie, 'for chewing on the textbooks!'

Go to page 64

THE BEST TEACHER IS THE ONE WHO ISN'T HERE...

'Crumbs!' says Rubi, looking at her watch. 'It's 9:30. Miss Mistry is really late! I hope nothing bad has happened.'

'Maybe there's a staff meeting,' says Jem. 'Stevie Star just sent a message to the group chat saying Mr Teacher hasn't turned up either, and he hasn't been late in 70 years! Stevie is in class 2B, by the way,' she adds to you.

'There was no one in the school office either,' you add, pleased to be able to join in.

'I'll send Billy to find out what's going on,' says Dennis. '**HEY, BILLY!**'

A boy sitting a couple of rows ahead stands up and . . .

. . . appears in front of you. He has a single spike of blond hair, right at the front of his head.

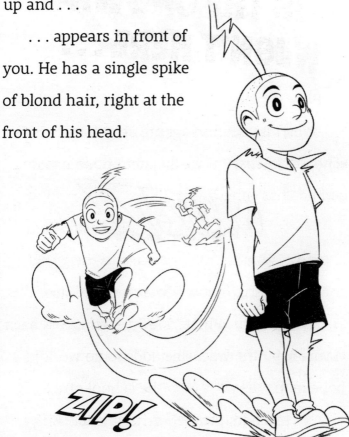

ZIP!

'We're wondering where Miss Mistry and Mr Teacher are,' Dennis says. 'Can you have a look round the school to see what's going on?'

Billy vanishes.

'Won't it take him ages to search the whole school?' you ask. 'If we all split up, we could . . .'

Billy is back.

'Who *is* that?' you whisper to Pie Face.

'That's Billy Whizz,' Pie Face whispers back. 'Some say he's the fastest kid in the world. I believe it.'

'No teachers. Anywhere in school,' Billy

says. 'Zero. Zip. Zilch. No office staff. No Olives. Only Ralf and Winston. Asleep in the janitor's cupboard. Took care of it, obvs.'

'Did you ask Ralf where the teachers are?' asks Rubi.

'No,' says Billy, dropping a big set of keys on her desk. 'I locked them in! **Tee-hee**!'

Dennis sits back and whistles.

'**OMG!**' he says. 'No teachers. No office staff. No dinner ladies. You know what this means, don't you?'

THE PUPILS ARE IN CHARGE OF BASH STREET SCHOOL!

Go to page 69

DENNIS MENACE AND THE THREE DARING PLANS!

'What if something bad has happened to the teachers?' asks Pie Face.

'I reckon they all just quit,' Minnie replies. 'I bet they arrived this morning, found out there was no milk in the staffroom fridge and decided that was the last straw.'

'Remember last Friday in assembly?' Dennis asks his friends. 'When we put drawing pins on some of the teachers' seats, and whoopee cushions on the rest?'

'The loudest assembly in history,' giggled
Jem. 'The roof nearly came off the school!'

'The teachers were pretty annoyed,'
admitted Dan. 'Maybe Minnie's right. Maybe
they've just had enough and quit, and this is
how school is going to be from now on. Just us.'

'**WOW!**' you say. 'I always tried to imagine what school would be like if the kids were in charge. Looks like I'm going to find out!'

'You certainly are!' a loud voice says.

It's Walter, and he's been listening in on your conversation.

AS THE MAYOR'S SON, IT'S MY DUTY TO TAKE CONTROL OF THE SCHOOL. I AM HERE TO INFORM YOU THAT I INTEND TO USE THIS POWER TO MAKE SOME IMPROVEMENTS AROUND HERE. YOU LOT PROBABLY WON'T LIKE IT, BUT I WILL, AND THAT'S ALL THAT MATTERS!

SHUT UP, WALTER. YOU COULDN'T TAKE CONTROL OF YOUR OWN UNDERPANTS!

'We'll see about that, Dennis,' says Walter, stalking back to where the Circle of Power are sitting obediently.

When Walter is out of earshot, Dennis waves everyone in for a huddle.

'Walter's right,' he says, almost blowing everyone's minds. 'Not about him taking over the school, of course, but about it being a chance to make school better. Imagine if WE could design a school from scratch,' Dennis suggests. 'It would be the best school EVER!'

'I'd put a slip and slide on every staircase,' says Minnie. 'And monkey bars above every toilet. Every bit of school should be more fun!'

'I'd improve the dinner menu,' says Pie Face. 'It would have every flavour pie you could ever want on it.'

'I'd make the school greener and try to reduce its carbon footprint,' says Vito.

'And more efficient,' adds Rubi. 'Imagine how much we could learn doing that!'

'Those are all great,' says Jem, 'but I think I'd like to make sure the teachers are really all OK first.'

'I can help you search,' Dan offers.

'What about you?' Dennis asks. 'What would you do?'

You think hard.

'I'd like to help all of you,' you say.

'Gnasher and I will keep an eye on Walter and his cronies,' says Dennis.

'Smart,' says Minnie, appreciatively. 'Let's team up. Vito and Rubi, you're Team Green, making the school greener. Jem and Dan are

Team Red, trying to find out what's happened to the teachers. Pie Face and I will be Team Yellow. We'll make school awesome – me with fun, you with food. Dennis and Gnasher can be Team Blue, making sure Walter doesn't do anything annoying.'

Minnie turns to you. 'And you can help us all,' she says. 'OK?'

'OK,' you hear yourself answer.

Your first Bash Street adventure is about to begin! **EEK!**

But who do you want to help first?

To help Team Green, go to page 81

To assist Team Red, go to page 100

EARNING YOUR RED AND BLACK STRIPES!

You don't really like other people deciding who you can be friends with, so you stand up and walk to the back of the class.

'Hi again,' says Dennis cheerfully. 'Had enough of the Circle of Power?'

'All I wanted to do was meet your friends, but they've as good as booted me out of the Circle for it,' you say, and introduce yourself to everyone.

'Forget Walter and his cronies,' interrupts

the red-haired girl sitting beside Dennis. You recognise her as the one who shouted out about the teachers before. 'I'm Minnie. I'm what you might call the supreme leader of this class, if not the whole school.'

You balk. This isn't another Circle of Power, is it?

'Minnie's my cousin,' grins Dennis. 'She talks a lot of rubbish.'

Minnie sticks her tongue out at him. You relax a bit.

'I'm Rubi,' says another red-haired girl, sitting in a wheelchair with all kinds of high-tech gizmos attached to it.

'Cool tech,' you remark.

'Thanks, I invented it all myself,' Rubi replies proudly.

'Rubi's a genius,' says a tall girl with dreadlocks. 'She can invent anything. I'm Jem, by the way.'

'Not anything,' Rubi argues, 'but most things, yes.'

'Awesome,' you say.

A black-haired girl wearing a green t-shirt with a big picture of the sun on it throws herself into the seat in front of Dennis's.

'Can you believe people are still putting paper in the plastic recycling bin?' she says. 'I had to sort it all or none of it would have been recycled properly!'

'This is Vito,' chuckles Dennis. 'She's all about saving the planet!'

'You can sit next to me if you like. The seat's free,' says Vito.

You glance over at where Walter has returned and is now glaring daggers at you. You thank Vito and sit down next to her.

'Pie Face,' says a boy wearing a yellow beanie. 'I mean me, not you, obviously. I'm not calling you a name.'

'The name's Badu,' says another boy. 'Dan Badu.'

'Nice tux,' you say.

'Dan's a spy,' says Pie Face between bites of what looks like a full-English pie.

'SHHHH! Enemy agents are everywhere! His eyes narrow on you for a moment.

'We've just been talking about The Situation,' says Dennis. 'I don't know if you heard, but all the teachers have disappeared.'

'I heard,' you reply. 'The Circle of Power know too.'

'I bet Walter already has an evil plan,' Dennis says.

'I don't know about evil, but he was just on the phone to his father,' you tell them.

Dennis and his friends all share a look. 'Definitely evil,' they all agree.

Go to page 69

TEAM GREEN!

'Ahh, great! You've joined us just in time,' says Rubi. 'Right, Vito?

'Yep,' agrees Vito. 'We're still figuring out what to do. I've been bugging Mrs Creecher for AGES to improve the school's carbon footprint and now is our chance to make a real change!'

Bash Street School's carbon footprint, before Vito gets to work! – The Ed

The three of you make your way to the Science Lab, which is right next door to Class 3C.

'OK,' you say. 'How can I help?'

'We need a renewable energy source,' says Vito. 'So we can reduce our carbon footprint, cut the bills and use the money for better things, such as more plants for outside to attract bees.'

'Right,' says Rubi. 'The school's heating still uses COAL, and that went out with the dinosaurs! Well, technically it was formed before the dinosaurs, but you know what I mean. But there's no point having clean heating if the heat is just going to escape. I think we should insulate the school first. Keep all the heat in, instead of wasting it.'

'We can do both,' you suggest. 'Why don't we try to insulate first and worry about clean energy after that?'

Vito and Rubi nod. You look around the lab. There's a lot of equipment, but not much in the way of useful insulation materials.

'We're going to need a lot of insulation,' says Rubi. 'There aren't enough materials here. We need industrial quantities of stuff we can mix up and stick to the outside of the building. And we'll need a way to spray it onto the walls as well!'

'I know a way we can spray it,' Vito says. 'I'll go and sort that out while you get the insulation ready.'

She runs out of the lab.

'It's up to us now,' Rubi says. 'But how are we going to make our insulation?'

You have an idea!

To check out the art room for supplies, go to page 85

To search the kitchen for ingredients, go to page 89

GET ARTY-FARTY!

'What about thick, gloopy paint?' you ask. 'Would that be any good as insulation?'

'That could work. Plus I heard Miss Daub needed feathers for a still-life drawing lesson and ordered ten kilograms of feathers instead of just ten feathers.'

'I'm sure we could mix up some insulation with those,' you say. 'My feather duvet keeps me nice and warm at night.'

'The art room is around the other side of the school,' says Rubi. 'Let's go!'

In the art storage cupboard, you find massive barrels of lovely thick paint in every colour under the sun, as well as bags upon bags stuffed with feathers.

Rubi sticks a finger into a barrel, then watches as the paint slooooooowly drips off.

'It's thick enough that this just might work! The feathers will stick right to it,' she says. 'This was a great idea!'

'And the school will look like a piece of art,' you laugh, 'painted all these different colours and covered in feathers!'

'Like a giant tropical bird!' Rubi laughs.

She frowns as something buzzes in her pocket. 'Someone's messaging me,' she says, pulling out her phone. 'It's Vito. She says she's got an insulation sprayer, and she'll send me a picture of it.'

The phone vibrates again. Rubi looks at the screen and gasps.

'UH-OH!'

'What is it?' you ask.

'We've got a problem!' says Rubi, showing you her phone.

On the screen you can see Vito has taken a selfie of her and . . .

'That's Ellis the elephant,' groans Rubi. 'His trunk is the perfect insulation sprayer, but we can't get him to suck up barrel-loads of paint – we don't know if it's safe and it will taste disgusting!'

YEUGH!

'You're right. This idea isn't going to work. Don't worry,' you say. 'Stay positive and we'll think of something else.'

You snap your fingers.

'I've got a sweet idea,' you say, grinning.

Go to page 89

GRUB'S UP!

'There will be loads of ingredients in the kitchen,' you say.

'Great idea!' says Rubi. 'Come on, let's check it out!'

You use the lift to go down to the ground floor, where the kitchen is.

'Both the dinner ladies are called Olive,' Rubi tells you. 'There's Olive Pratt and Olive Sprat. And they have this massive storage cupboard for ingredients.'

Rubi is right. The storage cupboard is jammed with ginormous sacks of lovely ingredients. You look around for something big enough to mix in. Outside, there's a giant bin, which is perfect. You give it a hose down so it's clean, and you're ready!

I THINK SIX SACKS OF INGREDIENTS WILL DO IT.

You choose six ingredients from the cupboard and the pair of you carry them all outside.

JELLY

CUSTARD

HUNDREDS & THOUSANDS

SEMOLINA

CABBAGE

GRAVY GRANULES

FISH SAUCE

TAPIOCA

BAKED BEANS

MAYONNAISE

DRIED BROCCOLI

CURRY POWDER

DEVILLED EGG POWDER

SPONGE CAKE

MASHED POTATO

PRUNE EXTRACT

FLOUR

OLIVE'S SPECIAL PILCHARD PUREE

COCOA

SUGAR

Just as you finish mixing in the final ingredient (with a cricket bat from the P.E. cupboard), someone, or rather something, clears its throat nearby.

You look up to find Vito standing there grinning beside a huge elephant.

'Something you'd like to spray?' Vito asks.

'ELLIS!' cries Rubi, zooming out to pat her pal – the elephant, not Vito! 'Ellis is always popping out of the zoo to visit us,' she tells you, scratching Ellis on the trunk.

'Well, we've got a treat for him today,' you say. Ellis's trunk snuffles at your pockets.

'No, in HERE!' you laugh, pointing at the bin.

Ellis's trunk reaches in and sniffs the mixture. His eyes widen and what looks like a smile creeps around the edges of his mouth.

'I've explained to Ellis what we want him to do,' says Vito. 'Elephants are super clever – smarter than most grown-ups – so I think this will work!'

'Suck it in and spray it out, Ellis!'

Will it stick? you wonder. *Please let it stick!*

It sticks! You, Rubi and Vito high-five each other.

Then you all high-five Ellis on the trunk.

'Ew! Sticky!' you cry.

'Great work, Team Green!' says Rubi. 'That's half of our mission accomplished!'

'Yeah,' says Vito. 'Now all we need is a clean source of energy and we'll have the greenest school in the world!'

At that moment, three kids from another class come over to marvel at the insulation-spraying elephant.

'Oh, hi, Ellis!' says a boy with scruffy black hair and a blue-and-black striped jumper. He gives the elephant an affectionate pat on the side

'Oh, I have to draw this!' says a girl wearing

a purple hijab with a butterfly clip. She pulls a tablet out of her bag and starts sketching Ellis spraying the school with slop.

'Wow, you're really talented!' you say.

'Thank you,' the girl says. 'I'm Sketch Khad, by the way. Are you new?'

'Started today!'

A girl with a red polka-dot bow perched on top of her head comes over. 'Welcome to Bash Street School! We're in class 2B. That over there is my twin brother, Sidney, and I'm Toots!'

'Toots? I've never met anyone called that before,' you say.

'My real name is Kate,' Toots explains. 'Toots is just my nickname, because of this . . .'

Toots lets out a high-pitched toot from her bottom. Everyone falls about laughing loudly, you included.

'That gives me an idea,' you say to Vito and Rubi.

'Let's hear it,' says Vito eagerly.

'What are the two most common types of renewable energy?' you ask.

'Solar and wind,' Rubi says quickly.

'But the sun doesn't always shine and the wind doesn't always blow,' Vito adds, 'so we'd need both.'

'Wait a minute,' you say. 'What if there's a kind of wind that always blows?'

'That would be amazing,' Rubi says, 'but unless we can control the weather, how does that help us?'

PARP!

'**ELLIS!**' exclaims Vito.

PHHHT!

'**SIDNEY!**' shouts Sketch.

TOOOT!

'Sorry,' says Toots. 'Honestly, just a sniff of the Olive's school dinners makes me need to fart!'

'Exactly!' you giggle. 'And, judging by the huge amount of baked beans in the kitchen cupboards, this whole school spends quite a bit of the day tooting and frooting! Am I right?' At least half of the cupboard had been full of giant tins of beans alone.

'You're not kidding!' Rubi laughs. 'Even the teachers can't help it!'

'You think we can harness the power of parp to run and heat the school?' exclaims Rubi. 'It might work . . .'

'Jem did say you can invent anything,' you say.

'Not anything . . . but maybe this. It will take a really cool new kind of turbine,' Rubi muses, pulling out a notebook, 'but I think I can see how it would work.'

'You're a genius! Come on,' says Vito. 'Let's go back to the lab and work it out together. Ellis will keep spraying the school – he's having a great time!'

'We'll keep an eye on him!' Sidney says. The other two nod in agreement, Sketch still scribbling away on her tablet.

'You two go back to the lab,' you say. 'I'm going to see if any of the other teams need any help.'

To go help Team Red find the teachers next, go to page 100

To go aid Team Yellow add fun to the school, go to page 120

Helped all the teams? Time to help Dennis and Gnasher on page 131

TEAM RED!

You find Jem and Dan rifling through a supply cupboard upstairs.

'I don't think the teachers are in there, Dan,' says Jem.

'Maybe there's a trapdoor somewhere,' Dan calls from within the cupboard. 'Or a portal. You just never know.'

'Can I help?' you ask.

'Of course!' says Dan.

Once you've helped Dan check the entire cupboard, the three of you head downstairs. Jem explains more about what Billy Whizz had seen earlier.

'He said he looked everywhere,' says Jem. 'He started on floor three, then down onto two, then down to one.'

'But he didn't check the basement,' says Dan. 'So that's where we should go next.'

'You're right,' Jem says. 'Maybe they were

having a team meeting down there and someone ate the custard cream propping the door open, and now they're trapped down there with no more biscuits.'

'What's that?' you ask, pointing to an old book Jem is carrying.

'This is Jem Jones's journal,' says Jem. 'My name is Jem Jones too, but that Jem Jones wrote this long before I was born. It's a record of all the spooky things she found in Beanotown. My mum recently handed it down to me – it's been in our family for generations. And there's more.'

She shows you an old key on a chain around her neck. 'This is the skeleton key. I can use it to trap ghosts and spirits, then imprison them in the journal forever.'

'**WOW!**' you say. 'Do you think something spooky has happened to the teachers?'

'Dunno,' says Jem, shrugging. 'The last time we thought something spooky was going on, it just turned out to be Lord Snooty's butler dressed up as a bogeyman. But maybe. The basement is weird.'

The basement IS weird. Dark, with deep shadows and lots of cobwebs. The lights flicker. There's a leak somewhere, dripping loudly into a puddle.

As you make your way along the corridor, you hold your breath.

Suddenly . . .

BANG! BANG! BANG!

You jump and hit your head on a pipe.
CLANG!

'It's just the boiler,' says Dan. 'It's ancient.'

Jem takes the skeleton key out again. She holds it up and turns around slowly. The key glows blue when she faces the boiler room, and dims when she turns away.

'Whatever's in there,' says Jem, 'the key reckons we should check it out!'

'You can find your ghoul later,' says Dan. 'We're looking for the teachers, remember?'

You try all the doors in the basement, one by one. They're all locked.

'They're not down here,' says Dan.

'We still haven't tried in there,' you say, pointing at the boiler room.

Dan steels himself and turns the handle on the boiler-room door, a finger to his lips. **'SHHH!'**

He throws the door open. The basement is filled with a fiery orange light, and the banging, clanging noises from the boiler get even louder.

You go into the boiler room and gasp. The boiler is . . . **alive!**

'It's beautiful!' says Jem, flicking through her journal.

She must have meant 'beautiful for a ghastly supernatural horror show', because the boiler is pretty ugly, even for a boiler.

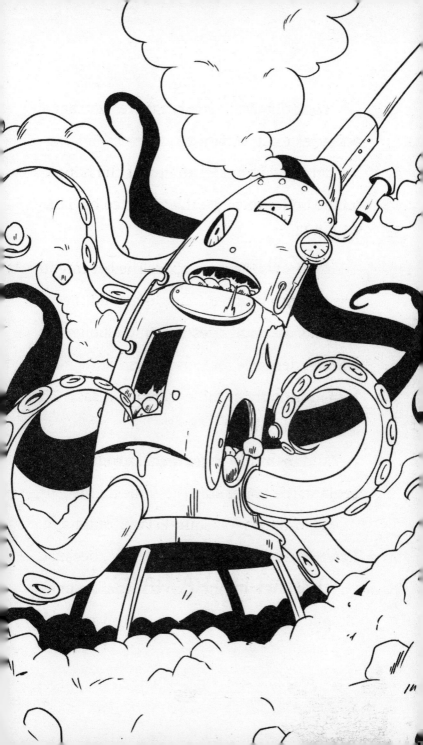

'Look out, Jem!' you cry, as two of the tentacles reach out for your new friend. But Jem is engrossed in her journal, and by the time she looks up it's too late – the tentacles grab her by the arms!

'**AARGH!**' Jem cries. 'Help me! I can't reach the skeleton key!'

'I'll save you!' cries Dan, racing forward. Another tentacle swoops around and grabs him around the middle, hoisting him into the air! '**AHH!**'

And then things get much, much worse. The beast in the boiler starts to *tickle* them!

'Woo-hoo-hoo!' squeals Dan. 'I give up! I give up!'

'**AAAAH-HA-HA-HA!**' cackles Jem. 'Stop it! Please! I'm going to wet myself!'

It's horrible! You look around. There's
nothing of any use . . . all you can see is a
fire hose on the wall. Then you notice Jem's

skeleton key swinging from its chain around her neck.

You know you need to make a decision, and fast – what are you going to do?

To grab the fire hose, go to page 111

To snatch the skeleton key, go to page 116

SUPER SPOOKY SOAKER!

'I've got a plan!' you shout, running over to the fire hose. You grab it by the nozzle and drag the heavy hose towards the boiler. One of its eyes swivels to look right at you, and suddenly three of its tentacles are shooting towards you!

'Look out!' cries Jem.

You turn the valve to switch on the water. It comes on with so much force that you're thrown back against the wall and pinned there. The water sprays over the boiler, turning instantly to steam, and blanketing the whole room in a thick, hot fog.

All you can see is Jem and Dan appearing then vanishing again as the tentacles thrash about, and the boiler's three eyes, which

have moved high above the steam to watch you. You squirt some water at the eyes and they duck back into the fog.

You direct the hose to where you think Jem is.

There's a loud shriek.

'UGH, THAT WATER'S COLD!'

'Sorry, Jem!' you cry.

You point the hose a little bit closer to the boiler, hoping to hit the tentacle that's holding onto her. There's another monstrous roar, this time from the beast, and Jem drops to the floor. The beast clearly doesn't like its tentacle being sprayed!

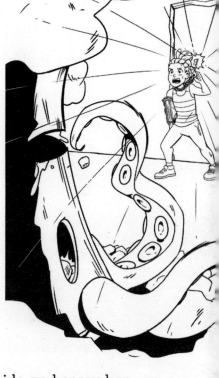

Spotting Jem, you aim the hose at her backside and spray her right out of the boiler-room door.

Then you turn the hose on where you think Dan is, set him free and wash him out of the door after Jem.

You drop the hose and sprint for the door, with a tentacle following you!

You almost make it, but then you feel the slimy tentacle wrapping round your leg. It's caught you!

'YOUR CHAPTER'S CLOSED!' Jem commands, thrusting out her journal.

The boiler lifts right off the floor, then explodes with bright, white light. You look away to protect your eyes, but you can see Jem guiding the protesting spirit towards the journal. The book glows. Jem picks it up and snaps it shut, *trapping the spirit inside.*

'Wow!' says Dan. 'That's quite a book, Jem.'

Jem tucks the journal under her arm and puts the chain holding the skeleton key back around her neck.

'Thanks,' she says to you. 'I'm not sure I could have stood much more tickling!'

'Are we done down here? This place gives me the creeps,' you ask.

'Let's go back upstairs!' Dan and Jem agree.

To go find Team Yellow next, go to page 120

Want to help Team Green next? Turn to page 81

Helped all the teams? Time to help Dennis and Gnasher on page 131

115

UNLOCKING THE SOLUTION!

You run towards Jem.

'Give me the key!' you shout.

Jem, who is being held upside down now, wriggles and thrashes about until the chain drops over her head.

'Hurry!' she cries.

You catch the key and hold it up as you saw Jem do outside the door. Nothing.

'It's not working,' you cry.

'Does it need to be charged or something?'

'I think it only works for people in my family,' groans Jem.

Dan drops to the floor.

'How did you get free?' you ask, astonished.

'I tickled it back!' says Dan.

'Tickle the tentacle, Jem!' you shout. 'It hates to be tickled!'

Jem runs her fingers over the tentacle, which shudders and then releases her. She drops to the floor with a THUD!

'Let's get out of here,' Dan cries, running for the door. You and Jem follow, Jem bending to retrieve her journal as she goes. You run as fast as you can, but one of the tentacles is gaining on you!

You dive through the door, then Jem follows suit.

'SHUT THAT DOOR!' you cry.

'Sorry!' Dan says to the boiler, before letting the tentacle withdraw and slamming the door shut behind it.

'I didn't mean to hurt it,' he says.

'PHEE-EW!' you say. 'We made it!'

'Yes, but the beast is still in there,' says

Jem. 'We need to catch it.'

'Leave it,' says Dan, brushing down his suit. 'We know the teachers aren't down here, so let's continue our search elsewhere.'

Jem looks longingly at the boiler-room door.

'OK,' she says, eventually.

'You can come back another time,' you say. 'Dan's right. We need to find the teachers.'

'They could be hiding outside somewhere,' Jem suggests.

'Perhaps there's a secret bunker beneath the school field!' says Dan.

'You guys go on without me. I'll go help some of the others,' you say.

To assist Team Green, go to page 81

To go find Team Yellow next, go to page 120

Helped all the teams? Time to help Dennis and Gnasher on page 131

TEAM YELLOW!

Class 3C isn't a happy place when you find Team Yellow there. Apart from Walter's area of it, at least. You approach Dennis, Gnasher, Minnie and Pie Face, who are huddled at the back of the classroom, watching the scene unfold with grim expressions.

'What's going on?' you ask.

'Nobody really knows,' says Minnie. 'Walter's trying to throw his weight around, and the Circle of Power keep looking out of the windows as if they're expecting something to happen. They've been distracting us from all our fun plans.'

'That's not good,' you say.

'NO TALKING,' shouts Walter from the front of the class, rapping on the whiteboard with a pointer. 'That's one of the new rules!'

There are six new rules written on the whiteboard in Bertie's blocky handwriting.

- NO TALKING
- NO LAUGHING
- NO PHONES (UNLESS THE MAYOR PHONES YOU ON IMPORTANT BUSINESS)
- NO PRANKS
- DO WHAT WALTER SAYS
- RESPECT THE CIRCLE OF POWER

'CRUMBS!' you say. 'Doesn't he know rules are made to be broken?'

'He's been finding that out,' chuckles Dennis. 'No one has been paying the slightest bit of attention to him. He's getting angrier by the minute!'

'I hope the teachers turn up soon,' says Pie Face. 'Right now, a school run by kids isn't actually all that much fun.'

'Cheer up,' you say. 'Why don't we start making it more fun right now?'

'Yeah!' Pie Face says, brightening. 'Are you ready, Minnie?'

'Always!' says Minnie. 'Come on!'

'I've been thinking about my pie plans all morning,' Pie Face says, as you leave the class.

'Where do you think you're going?' Walter calls after you. 'You have to ask me if you want to leave the room!'

Minnie stops, turns around and . . .

RAZZZZZ!

'That told him!' laughs Pie Face.

'What are we going to do, then?' you ask. 'What's the plan?'

'My plan is to make every bit of school more fun,' says Minnie.

'And I want to bake the biggest pie you've ever seen – big enough to feed the entire school,' says Pie Face.

'Okay, let's start with my first ingenious plan: to replace all the staircases with slip and slides,' Minnie says. 'Sound good?'

'Maybe you should add slides to the stairs instead of replacing them completely,' you suggest. 'It's hard to get up a slip and slide.'

'Good thinking!' says Minnie, rubbing out and rewriting. 'There are the lifts, but they take too long.'

'Won't slip and slides be expensive?' you ask. You didn't bring any money.

'Plug from 2B does a great impression of the mayor,' chuckles Minnie. 'He'll just phone up and tell the company to come, and send the bill to him! Class 2B are in the year below us,' she tells you. 'I'm like their hero. They'll do anything I ask. I call them Minnie's Minions!'

'We need more fun ideas!' says Pie Face. 'Have you got any more, Minnie?'

'As a matter of fact, I have made a list in my comic diary.' Minnie pulls a small book out of her hat and opens it up to the back page. She shares her list with you and Pie Face.

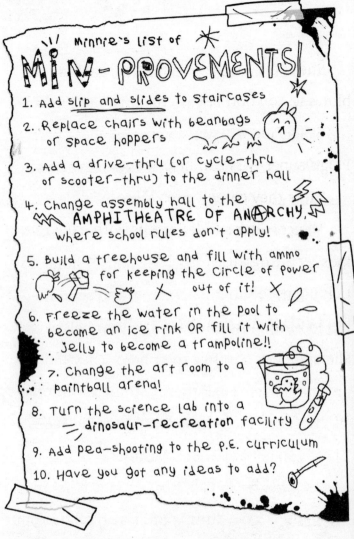

Minnie's list of

MIN-PROVEMENTS!

1. Add slip and slides to staircases

2. Replace chairs with beanbags or space hoppers

3. Add a drive-thru (or cycle-thru or scooter-thru) to the dinner hall

4. Change assembly hall to the AMPHITHEATRE OF ANARCHY, where school rules don't apply!

5. Build a treehouse and fill with ammo for keeping the Circle of Power out of it!

6. Freeze the water in the pool to become an ice rink OR fill it with jelly to become a trampoline!!

7. Change the art room to a paintball arena!

8. Turn the science lab into a dinosaur-recreation facility

9. Add pea-shooting to the P.E. curriculum

10. Have you got any ideas to add?

'That's probably enough for one day,' says

Minnie. 'Time to get 2B on the case!'

She takes a whistle from her sleeve and blows it. You don't hear anything.

'It's a Plug whistle,' Pie Face explains. 'Only Plug's super-ears can hear it.'

'Here they come!' cries Minnie.

The corridor suddenly fills with excitable kids, chatting and laughing and shoving and tickling each other.

'QUIIIIIIIIET!' yells Minnie, silencing them immediately.

'This is class 2B,' she says, pointing to each kid in turn. 'Plug, Danny, Freddy, Harsha, Stevie, Erbert, Smiffy, Scotty, Mandi, Wilfrid and Mahira. Hang on. Where's Toots, Sidney and Sketch?'

The gang of kids all look at each other and shrug.

'Cuthbert is still crying and hugging Mr Teacher's empty seat,' says a boy in a black jumper with a yellow skull and crossbones on it. Minnie rolls her eyes. 'Hi, I'm Danny. You must be the new kid.'

You wave hello. Minnie rips the list out of her comic diary and hands it over to Danny.

'I want all these things done, please. If you need money,' she adds, winking mischievously at a boy with handle-bar ears,

who must be Plug, 'the mayor will cover
the bill.'

Plug salutes with a chuckle. 'You're the
boss!' he says.

'Do any of you know how I can bake
a pie big enough to feed the entire school?'
Pie Face asks.

'I bet one of my followers will have an
idea,' Stevie Star replies, already filming a live
video on one of his social media accounts.

The kids from 2B break up into groups to
complete the tasks Minnie has set them, with
Freddy, Stevie and Mahira joining Pie Face for
his pie-normous task.

'It seems as though you guys have got this
covered,' you say. 'I'll go help the others.'

To go help Team Red, go to page 100

To go help Team Green, go to page 81

Helped all the teams? Time to help
Dennis and Gnasher on page 131

TEAM BLUE!

When you walk back into Class 3C, you find it empty. There's no sign of Walter or the rest of the Circle of Power, and no sign of Dennis or his friends.

'Pssst,' comes a noise from the corner of the classroom, where Dennis is hiding behind a skeleton model.

You go over to the windows and look out. Below, a fleet

of yellow vehicles are driving into the school grounds. There are diggers, trucks and tractors.

'This doesn't look good,' you say. 'What's Walter up to?'

'We don't know,' says Dennis. 'Billy's gone to see if he can find out.'

'Maybe he's building an adventure playground,' you say hopefully. 'Or an epic go-kart track?'

'I don't think so,' says someone beneath the desk next to you, making you jump.

You peer under the table.

'This is Roger.' Dennis introduces you.

'Walter thinks like a greedy grown-up,' Roger says, getting up. 'To figure out what he's doing, we need to try to think that way too.'

'It will be something to do with money,' says Dennis. 'And making himself richer and more powerful. He'll do anything to achieve that goal.'

WHOOSH!

Billy Whizz appears by your side from nowhere, almost frightening you to death.

'Walter's digging up the playground!' he says. 'Once it's been dug up, they're going to drill for oil, dig for coal and frack for gas. Walter reckons he can make millions by selling the energy back to the school for years to come!'

'No, no, no!' Vito groans as she enters the room with Rubi. 'That's the last thing we need! The fart turbine Rubi and I developed will mean the school doesn't need any fossil fuel at all!'

'Walter won't care about that, will he?' Dennis says grimly.

The others, minus Pie Face, enter the classroom, having completed their missions. Dennis fills everyone in on what's going on.

'We have to stop him,' Dan says. 'But how?'

'Remember when Lord Snooty tried to build an art gallery in the grounds of Bunkerton Castle?' Minnie asks. 'When they were digging the foundations, they found those remains of King Boris III, and they had to stop so archaeologists could do a proper excavation.'

'That's right,' says Jem. 'Snooty didn't mind, so he just let them get on with it and opened his gallery somewhere else.'

'But if something valuable turned up under the playground, they'd have to stop digging there too!' cried Dennis.

'What's going to turn up under the playground, though?' asks Roger.

'Anything we put out there,' grinned Dennis. 'Maybe the remains of Queen Doris?'

'What about this skeleton?' you say, holding up its bony arm and waving it.

WHY DOES ONE NOT WATCH SCARY MOVIES? BECAUSE ONE DOESN'T HAVE THE GUTS!

'And there's a crown and velvet robe in the drama cupboard,' says Dan. 'That's all we'd need to make a pretty convincing royal fossil.'

'That's Plan A, then,' says Minnie. 'What about Plan B?'

'Nobody needs a Plan B when Plan A is this good!' snorts Dennis.

'Yes, they do!' says Rubi. 'You should always have a Plan B!'

'How about . . .' you say, 'we pretend to be aliens invading Earth? That will surely scare them off!'

'There's paint and feathers in the art cupboard. I'm sure we could make a convincing alien,' Rubi adds.

Minnie grins. 'That's my kind of plan. Can we call it Plan M?'

Dan looks at you. 'There's one more idea,' he says mysteriously. 'You could go undercover as a secret agent and mess up Walter's plan from the inside.'

'**What?** I could never pull that off!' you scoff.

Dennis looks thoughtful. Rubi takes a picture of him with her phone.

'What gives?' he asks.

'I've never seen you looking thoughtful before,' she laughs. 'I wanted proof!'

'Whatev's,' says Dennis. 'Dan's idea could be worth a try. Walter doesn't know you very well yet. He might be convinced to trust you.'

'I could try,' you say nervously.

'Great, we'll call that one Plan D for Dan – and Dennis, because I approved it,' says

Dennis. 'So we've got Plan A, Plan M and we've got Plan D. The question is, which one should we try first?'

'You make pretty good choices,' Minnie says to you. 'What do you think?'

If you think you should try Plan A and bury the skeleton, go to page 139

If you think you should try Plan M and dress up as an alien, go to page 151

You think you should try Plan D and go spy on the Circle of Power, go to page 164

PLAN A –
THE RIB-TICKLER!

'Plan A seems a bit easier to believe,' you say, 'so Walter might just fall for it.'

'Plan A it is!' cries Dennis, clapping his hands. 'Jem, Rubi, Roger – you go and get some paint from the art room, this skeleton needs to look a lot older. Dan, Vito and Minnie – you hit the drama cupboard and see what royal bits and pieces you can find in there. We'll meet at the kitchen doors in five minutes.'

When they've left, Dennis shakes his head.

'Of all the nasty things to do, digging up a

playground must be one of the worst,' he says. 'We all have so much fun out there!'

'Don't worry, Dennis,' you say. 'We'll stop him. It's a good plan.'

'I just hope we can pull it off. I'm glad you're here to help us.' He shoots you a smile.

'Come on, let's go down to the kitchen and see what's happening outside,' you say.

What's going on outside is lots of noisy stuff. A digger is breaking up the concrete of the playground, while a tractor scoops it up and deposits it on a dump truck.

The others join you, bringing their finds with them.

You dress the skeleton in a purple velvet robe, gold chain and crown, then put golden rings on its bony fingers.

'Very regal,' says Minnie admiringly.

'How are we going to get it into the hole they're digging without them seeing us?' you ask.

'That's the easy bit,' says Dennis. 'I've arranged for Ice Ice Betty's ice cream van to go past in a minute. When her van drives by playing her dope beats, those workers will all look up. And that's when Billy here will sneak the queen into the hole.'

Sure enough, you can soon hear Ice Ice Betty approaching, the booming from her bass bins moving from ear-tickling to earth-trembling as she gets closer. But you realise that the

vibrations are not just from the music alone, but the dancing elephant following her. *Ellis!*

Soon the sounds are loud enough for the workers to hear through their ear defenders, and they shut off their machines and run to watch the spectacle and join the queue. You couldn't ask for a better distraction!

'Now, Billy!' you cry. Billy grabs the skeleton, vanishes, then returns without it quicker than you can say 'where did he go?'.

Walter is disgusted to see his workers abandoning their stations to buy anything so childish as an ice cream. As for that elephant, he must tell Bertie to go find it for him. It could be useful . . .

'Get back to work!' he cries, waving the workers away from the ice cream van.

Grumbling, they return to their machinery, hardly noticing the group of kids looking into the hole they're digging and pointing at something, until one of them waves.

HEY! YOU'D BETTER COME AND LOOK AT THIS!

The workers wander over to see what all the fuss is about. Walter stomps over to tell his workers off for being distracted and not getting back to work.

'What is it now?' he blusters.

Rubi points to the muddy skeleton at the bottom of the hole.

'Congratulations! Your workers have unearthed a priceless piece of history!' she says excitedly. 'This is the long-lost resting place of Queen Doris of Beanotown.'

Walter gulped.

'Don't worry,' says Dennis, pointing to his phone. 'I've already reported your valuable discovery to the museum. They say their best expert will be here in half an hour once he's finished his noodles.'

'It's **VERY** illegal to tamper with something as important as this,' you say. 'So it looks like your digging will have to stop, Walter.'

'We'll see about that,' says Walter, jumping into the hole. 'Hey Gnasher, you filthy little hound! Look at this lovely pile of juicy old bones! I bet they're yummy!'

'**OH NO!**' Dennis gasps.

A million years of evolution is pounding away in Gnasher's doggy brain, telling him that bones are juicy and delicious, and he doesn't know when he'll get another one. Even if he knows full well that they are fake.

It is hopeless. Gnasher leaps into the hole, grabs 'Queen Doris' by the ankle and flees.

'No, Gnasher, no!' cries Minnie.

Walter climbs out of the hole.

'No bones, no queen,' he says, dusting off his hands.

'Come on, back to your machines!' he says to the workers, who were all by now licking double 99s.

Gloom settles over your friends. The whole playground is soon going to look like this corner, all torn up and no fun.

A furious trumpeting sound lifts the mood. It's Ellis, and he looks a little . . . bloated. Well, more bloated than he usually looks.

'UH-OH!' said Vito. 'Did someone give Ellis ice cream?'

One of the workers sheepishly raises his hand.

'You fool!' cries Vito. 'Ellis is lactose intolerant! If he eats anything with dairy in it . . . well, you don't wanna be around when . . .'

BLAAART

Ellis farts so hard and so loudly that all four of his feet lift off the ground. That's 5,000 kilograms of elephant lifted into the air like a feather. What's worse is that the poor workers are right in the farting line and get a full-face gust of elephant gut-gas.

Turning green, the workers run, coughing, spluttering and maybe thinking that they had no idea this was going to be one of the worst days of their lives.

It's the funniest thing you've ever seen. Funnier even than the time your dad split his shorts playing crazy golf.

'Look!' cries Rubi, pointing at the roof of the school. 'Ellis's belly-blast has got my new turbines going! The school is officially running on fart gas! HOORAY!'

The only person not cheering is grumpy Walter. He stomps off back to class, and the rest of you follow.

You can't believe how much fun Bash Street School is turning out to be!

Go to page 180

PLAN M – IT'S OUT OF THIS WORLD!

'The good thing about Plan M is that it will probably scare Walter right out of his underpants,' you say.

'We're going to need an alien,' says Minnie. 'A really scary one!'

'Don't the tunnels under the school run beneath the playground?' asks Jem.

'What tunnels?' you ask.

Dennis grins. 'There are ancient tunnels beneath the school that you get to through a trapdoor in the basement. They run right below where Walter's stooges are digging.'

'Ooh, so could our alien rise up out of the ground right in front of them when they dig through?' you ask eagerly.

'I like the way you're thinking!' says Minnie. 'Rubi, we need a really loud and spooky voice for our alien too.'

'I can make a voice changer,' says Rubi. 'And I can integrate a speaker and a smoke machine. How does that sound?'

'AMAZING!' says Dennis. 'I can't wait to see Walter's face when this happens!'

'I think I would make a good alien,' you say, grinning. 'Especially with Gnasher sitting on my shoulders!'

'Vito and I will go get the paint and feathers,' Jem says.

The basement is dark and spooky, and gives you the creeps. Dennis finds the light switch and suddenly it's not so scary anymore. He leads you to a trapdoor hidden beneath a slop bucket in a cupboard. Dennis opens it, and Vito gets to work painting your face blue, while Minnie threads feathers into your hair and

Rubi straps her latest invention to your chest.

'Just speak into the microphone to change your voice and make it louder,' Rubi explains, 'and press the button to switch the smoke effects on.'

'Up, Gnasher!' says Dennis. Gnasher climbs up your body and perches on your shoulders, gripping you around the head. Vito puts a pair of lab safety goggles on him and a hard hat that Minnie had 'borrowed' from the workers, covered in feathers. She then fastens a space cloak over your head – a huge sheet of tinfoil Pie Face has given them from the kitchen, where he is still deliberating which filling he wants to make for his giant pie.

'Er, I can't see now,' you say.

'It's OK, Gnasher will tell you which way to walk,' says Dennis. 'You'd better go. You remember what to do?'

You nod. Gnasher grips your head harder, so he doesn't fall off your shoulders.

You start to walk. Gnasher slaps you on the left cheek, so you turn left.

'That's it,' you hear Dennis say. 'You're almost at the . . .'

OOF!

'I fell down the trapdoor, didn't I?' you call.

'Sorry!' says Dennis.

Gnasher pierces two small holes in the tin foil, just big enough to see where you're going.

'Good boy,' you say.

You and Gnasher make your way awkwardly through the tunnels beneath Bash Street School.

The tunnels are weird. They're lit by flaming torches and strange writing is carved into the walls. Gnasher slaps you on your

cheeks when you need to turn right or left, even though you can see now.

'You do remember I can see now, don't you? You can stop hitting me.'

'Gnee-hee!' giggles Gnasher.

The cheeky dog leads you through the tunnels to a door with a sign on it. *The Confiscatorium?* you think. *What's that?*

What's even stranger is that, once you go through the door, you meet a boy who looks exactly like Dennis, only he's wearing a Viking helmet, and he has a dog who looks almost exactly like Gnasher! If Dennis's Gnasher wasn't currently sat upon your head, you might even think that the Viking boy before you IS Dennis. Do Dennis and Gnasher both have twins? He didn't mention it . . .

Looking farther up the tunnel, you see that the workers have already managed to break through from above.

'Er, hi!' you say to Viking Dennis. 'Dennis says is it okay if we use your fizzy-pop elevator, whatever that means?'

'Of course,' says the boy. He even sounds just like Dennis. 'Be my guest.'

Gnasher leads you over to what looks like a piece of metal on top of a bucket of fizzy pop, positioned just below the hole in the tunnel ceiling and signals you to step up.

'Is this safe?' you ask, climbing on.

The Viking boy just shrugs. 'Say hi to Dennis for me,' says the Viking boy, pouring what looks like a bag full of chewy mint sweets into the fizzy pop below you.

Gnasher grips on tighter to your head. It must be show time!

WHOOOOSH!

The fizzy pop beneath the metal shoves you upwards! Up, up, until you shoot right out of the ground and into the daylight. You look around and see Walter and the workers.

You press the first button on the box tied to your chest. Smoke pours from beneath your cloak. You press the second button to activate the voice changer and speaker.

'I AM ENIGMATA, LORD OF PLANET ENIGMA!' you shout.

Your voice is so loud and creepy it almost scares you.

'I LANDED ON EARTH THOUSANDS OF YEARS AGO AND WAS ENJOYING A NICE, LONG NAP UNTIL YOU DISTURBED ME!'

You're enjoying it now.

'LEAVE OR I WILL CALL DOWN MY NASTY SPACE ARMY TO THIS PUNY PLANET AND BLOW UP THE NICEST HOUSE IN THIS TOWN.'

You point at Walter. 'YOUR HOUSE!'

Walter is terrified.

'I-I-I-M SORRY!' he gabbles, and then there's an enormous TWANG!

Walter's underpants fly right out of his trousers and into the air.

It's too much for Walter. With a wail, he flees the playground and heads for home. The Circle of Power looks at you, screams, then runs after Walter.

'Wait for us, Walter!' The fizzy pop runs out and you slowly lower back into the tunnel below. Dennis and your friends are crowding around you and crying with laughter.

TWANG

'I TOLD YOU WE'D SCARE WALTER OUT OF HIS UNDERPANTS!' you boom.

Whoops! You realise you're still speaking into the microphone.

Go to page 180

PLAN D – I SPY!

'It's a tough choice, but I think Plan D is the best way to save the playground,' you say.

'Spoken like a true Bash Street Kid,' Minnie says, with a big grin. 'Make sure you agree with everything Walter says.'

'Yes, he likes that,' adds Dennis. 'And say how important his dad— no, his *father* is.'

'Tell him his briefcase makes him look grown up,' says Roger, giggling.

'Shh!' hissed Rubi, gesturing towards the door. 'They're back!'

'OK!' you say. 'I think I'm ready to take down the Circle of Power!'

You stand up and stroll back to the front of the class where the Circle of Power have reappeared. Walter glares at you.

'Finished fraternising with the class delinquents?' he demands. 'It's too late to join the Circle of Power, you know.'

You pull your best disappointed face.

'You're right, Walter,' you say. 'I've no right to expect to be friends with anyone who has a father as important as yours.'

Walter's face softens, then he folds his arms. 'Well, I see you realise what a big mistake you've made.'

'I do,' you agree. 'But before I give up on the Circle forever, can I ask a question?'

165

'I suppose so,' says Walter.

'Where did you get your briefcase?' you ask. 'It makes you look so grown up, and I'd love to get something similar . . . but not as good as yours, obviously.'

Walter lays a hand on his briefcase. 'I'm sorry, but my father had it made specially for me. It's a one-off.'

'As are you, Walter,' you say, making your eyes as big as you can, then turning away.

'Let's not be so hasty,' cries Walter. 'I'll give you one last chance to be in the Circle of Power, on one condition – you never speak to those oiks again!'

'It's a deal!' you say.

Walter looks pleased. 'Your first mission for the Circle of Power is to guard the playground and stop Dennis and his friends from getting anywhere near the workers digging it up. I don't want anything disrupting their work. Bertie will help you. Got it?'

You nod. Bertie gets to his feet, half-tucks his shirt in and salutes Walter.

MISSION ACCEPTED!

Go to page 168

SECRET AGENT

You and Bertie take up your lookout positions in the playground. You share your favourite jokes and you start to think that Bertie is actually quite a good laugh.

'How do you think it's going?' you ask.

Which one is you, and which one's Bertie? — The Ed

'Slowly,' says Bertie. 'Walter's dad must have skimped on the machinery. The workers are doing a lot of the carrying by hand.'

That's good, you remind yourself, but progress isn't nearly slow enough! It needs to be halted.

'Walter won't be pleased,' Bertie says. 'He likes everything to be done by big noisy machines because that's the fastest way to smash things up.'

'Why are you friends with him?' you blurt. Bertie seems far too kind to be part of the Circle of Power.

'Walter's not so bad, you know. Sure, he's bossy, but he's also generous with his friends. You should see his home cinema room! There are definite perks to being in his circle.'

You didn't know about the cinema room . . .
No, you think, *Walter is destroying the playground. He needs to be stopped, cinema room or not.*

You watch as an elephant is led around the corner of the school, then starts spraying something disgusting and gloopy onto the school walls.

'Is that an actual elephant?' you ask Bertie, 'or am I imagining things?'

'That's Ellis,' says Bertie. 'He's always escaping. I don't know what he's doing with Rubi and Vito though.'

'To me, it looks like he's trying to insulate the building with school dinners,' you say.

Bertie snorts with laughter. 'That's so stupid. It smells like trifle!'

'It's actually pretty smart. The insulation will keep the energy inside the building and save on heating costs,' you tell him. 'It will make the school greener.'

Bertie frowns as if he doesn't quite understand the point. He turns back to the playground. 'What the workers need is some heavy-lifting equipment,' he says, thinking.

'What if we could persuade those kids to let Ellis help with that?' you ask, a plot forming in your mind.

'They don't like Walter, so I don't think they would go for it,' he says, 'but it would be cool.'

'You stay here and guard the site. I'll go and speak to them,' you say. 'Maybe they'll do a favour for the new kid.'

You make your way over to where Rubi and Vito are delightedly watching as Ellis squirts something that looks yucky but smells tasty onto the school.

'How's it going?' asks Rubi quietly.

'Good,' you whisper. 'Walter asked me and Bertie to guard the playground, so he trusts me. That's the good news.'

'What's the bad news?' asks Vito.

'The hole in the playground is getting bigger,' you say. 'I have an idea to stop it completely, but I'd need to borrow Ellis. Would that be OK?'

'Sure,' says Vito. 'He'll do anything for a peanut, but he's petrified of mice.'

'Excellent!' you say, grinning. 'Here's what I need you to do for me . . .'

Bertie grins as you lead Ellis towards the growing hole in the school playground.

'This should speed things up a bit,' you say, and put Ellis to work lifting the chunks of playground concrete

out of the hole and throwing them into the dump truck to be taken away.

'Walter is going to love you,' says Bertie. 'You'll probably even replace me as his number one friend.'

'Why?' you ask. 'Surely he wouldn't replace one of his oldest and most loyal friends with a complete newbie?'

'He definitely would,' says Bertie. 'He does it all the time. That's why Dudley and Susan are always competing to do stuff for him.'

You feel a bit sorry for Bertie. He has some good jokes and he laughs really loudly at yours too. He's a good friend.

Out of the corner of your eye, you catch sight of a little black creature zooming across the playground towards the workers. The creature has wiry black fur, big teeth and giant ears and whiskers. It's Gnasher, wearing a really, really bad mouse disguise!

'SQUEAK!'

screeches Gnasher.

'SQUEEEEEEEEK!'

This is awful, you think. No one will believe that Gnasher is a . . .

'MOUSE!' yells Bertie. 'A big, black mouse! Look out, Ellis!'

Ellis turns lazily from his work, then freezes. His eyes grow big and wild, he trumpets and then he starts to run.

Gnasher runs right, so Ellis runs left, smashing into the digger.

Gnasher runs left, so Ellis runs right, scattering all the workers.

You'll gnever forget this!

Gnasher runs round and round in circles, so Ellis goes absolutely berserk, jumping from one piece of equipment to another, sending nuts, bolts and hydraulic pipes flying everywhere.

You take a peanut out of your pocket and wave it at Ellis. The elephant stops. You wink at Gnasher, who runs back towards the school and disappears.

'Want a peanut, Ellis?' you ask. Ellis nods and takes the peanut gratefully.

You take Ellis back to Rubi and Vito.

'That was genius!' Rubi says.

'And hilarious!' adds Vito.

'Thanks for letting me pinch your pal,' you say, and head back to where Bertie is staring forlornly at the smashed-up digging equipment. You feel a bit bad for him.

'Where are the workers?' you ask.

'They left,' he says.

'That wasn't such a good idea of mine, after all,' you say. 'Will Walter be angry?'

'Don't worry,' he says. 'He'll blame me. He always does.'

'I don't know how you put up with him,' you say. 'You could be friends with anyone in class 3C.'

Bertie looks at you. 'I know,' he says, 'but if I'm not Walter's best friend then who would he have? No one else likes him. I don't know if you noticed, but he can be a real pain in the artichokes.'

You giggle. 'Pain in the artichokes?'

Bertie laughs. 'I made it up. It just sounds funny to me.'

'Sounds funny to me too,' you say.

Bertie takes out his mobile phone.

'Better tell Walter what happened,' he says.

You feel a bit sorry for Bertie, but you can't help but notice he doesn't seem to care about the fracking being stopped.

'Blame everything on me,' you say. 'I'm not sure that the Circle of Power is the right fit for me anyway.'

Bertie looks disappointed, but thanks you for taking the fall.

'Let's just go back to class,' you say. 'We can tell each other jokes while we go.'

Go to page 180

BACK TO 3C!

When you get back to 3C, Dennis shares with the class what just happened for those who weren't watching. The kids all cheer – except for the Circle of Power, of course – but Billy has a question.

'What about the teachers? Did you find them?' he asks.

'No, we didn't,' Jem admits. 'We sort of forgot about them.'

'Ahem!' says Angel Face, looking ever so slightly guilty. 'I, er, found a clue and solved that little mystery ages ago.'

'Well?' demands Minnie. 'Spill the beans, Angel Face!'

'I went to the office to look for clues,
and I found Mrs Creecher's to-do list.
There was an item on the list that looked like it
had been ticked off, but actually there was just
a smudge of haggis over the tick box.'

'And what was the item?' you ask.

'It said: "Email parents about teacher

training day" and the date was today,' says Angel Face. 'And then below it said: "Book paintball for staff away day" for today as well.'

The class is silent.

'So we didn't have to be here at all today?' asks Minnie.

'Pretty much,' says Angel Face. 'Anyway, the teachers are fine, so it's no biggy.'

YOU MEAN THE TEACHERS AREN'T MISSING?

THEY'RE PAINTBALLING AND DIDN'T INVITE US?

'No biggy?' cries Rubi. 'It's three o'clock! The teachers will be back in a minute and there are slip and slides in every stairway, the playground has been dug up and there's an elephant causing mayhem after covering the school in mixed-up school dinners!'

'CRUMBS! And I didn't even have time to finish my pie,' says Pie Face.

'We're really in for it now!' says Dan.

'We need to clean up the mess!' cries Vito.

'No,' says Dennis. 'To the tunnels! We can just say burglars did it!'

What do you want to do?

> To escape to the tunnels, go to page 184

> To clean up the mess, go to page 194

TO THE SECRET TUNNELS UNDER THE SCHOOL!

'There's no time to tidy up!' shouts Billy Whizz from the window.

You all rush to look out.

'No prizes for guessing who won! Miss Mistry's done us proud,' whispers Minnie. All the teachers are climbing out of a minibus, covered in paint splats except for a young teacher you assume must be Miss Mistry, who is spotlessly clean and looking massively smug.

'Follow me!' Dennis cries, leading the

charge to the basement and a trapdoor that leads to the tunnels.

Deep below the school, you creep through the tunnels, marvelling at the pictures and signs on the walls.

'This way,' Dennis says. 'This tunnel leads all the way to Beanotown-on-Sea. We'll be home before our parents even leave the house to get us.'

GROWL!

'Was that you, Gnasher?' asks Dennis.

It wasn't. But the high, angry yowling and gnashing that comes next is.

'Gnash gnash gnash!' gnashed Gnasher.
'Gnash gnash gnash!'

'What's got into him?' asks Minnie. 'The teachers will hear us if he doesn't pipe down.'

You point to the far end of the corridor.

'That's what's got into him,' you say, trembling. 'Alligators – and they're coming to eat us!'

'Not alligators – sewer-gators,' says Rubi, correcting you. 'But you're right about them coming to eat us!'

'Everybody get back to the school!' cries Dennis.

The stampede is so madcap that you can't help laughing as you run. No matter what happens now, this is still the best day you've ever had at school!

At the trapdoor, you help lift everyone up and out, and slam it shut just in the nick of time. You can hear the sewer-gators growling and prowling below.

'That was close!' you laugh. 'But we managed to get away!'

'Not quite!' says a voice you haven't heard before. When you look up, you see a small woman wearing large glasses and a very, very stern expression on her face.

'Hello, Mrs Creecher,' says Dennis. 'Did you enjoy paintballing?'

SEWER NICE TO SEE YOU!

'I did,' says your new headteacher. 'And now I'd like someone to explain why you kids are here and WHY my school is covered in revolting gruel?'

188

Nobody thinks they'll get detention on their first day at a new school.

And nobody dreams the whole school will get detention!

Mrs Creecher ordered everyone to clean the 'disgusting mess' off the school, and to put things back the way they were before she went paintballing, and that's why you're all scraping something that looks a bit like trifle off the wall.

'This is going to take weeks!' says Vito. 'Whose silly idea was this again?'

'I think it was yours,' you giggle.

'I wish there was a hungry beast that would just eat all this stuff off the walls,' says Rubi.

'Maybe there is,' you say, dropping your scraper and picking up a big blob of insulating slop. 'Wait here!'

You run into the school, and down the stairs into the basement. At the trapdoor, you listen for a second . . . good, you can hear the sewer-gators down there.

You lift the trapdoor and let a little bit of the slop fall down through it.

GOBBLE!

The gators go wild for your gruesome gateau. Perfect!

This crazy plan might just work, you think.

You make a trail by dropping little bits of trifle on the floor and make your way back to where your class is scraping the walls.

'Everybody out of the way!' you cry.

Your friends look at you, then at the hungry sewer-gators following you, and get out of the way. Five hungry sewer-gators can't believe their luck and throw themselves at the wall, licking and chewing and picking the food off the school.

'Well, that's not bad for your first day,' says Dennis admiringly. 'Have you learned anything at this crazy school?'

'Just one thing,' you say. 'In Beanotown,

no matter how much trouble you're in, if you stay positive and look hard enough, you will always find a way out!'

THE END

TIME TO CLEAN UP!

'If the teachers see everything we've done to the school, they'll throw a wobbly!' you say. 'We have to clean up the mess we've made!'

'What, all of it?' asks Dennis.

'Ellis has just finished spraying the insulation onto the school,' protests Rubi.

'I think it's warmer already,' says Vito.

'If Ellis likes squirting stuff on walls, he can wash it all off again with water!' you say. 'The rest of us need to get the school tidy!'

Not one of you has ever worked this hard in your lives. All over the school, kids are scrubbing things, fixing things, putting

things back and hiding the rest. Billy Whizz does most of the work, zooming around, stuffing things in cupboards and under desks. He also unlocks Ralph's door and finds the old janitor fast asleep in his chair – right where he left him.

Rodger the Dodger is on guard duty, watching at the window.

'Here they come!' he cries. You run over to see the teachers coming in through the front door of the school.

'No prizes for guessing who won! Miss Mistry's done us proud,' whispers Minnie. All the teachers are covered in paint splats except for a young teacher you assume must be Miss Mistry, who is spotlessly clean and looking massively smug.

'Time for us to be somewhere else!' shouts Dennis.

You drop what you're doing and run.

It's too late. Before you can get to the stairs leading to the pupils' exit, you all meet Miss Mistry in the corridor, along with a small woman wearing large glasses and a very, very stern expression. You assume this must be the head teacher, Mrs Creecher.

'Hello, class! What are you doing in school?' asks Miss Mistry. Then she catches sight of

you and gets distracted. 'Oh, hello. You must be my new pupil!' she says warmly.

'Did you enjoy your teacher training day?' asks Dennis innocently.

'Miss Mistry enjoyed it,' says Mrs Creecher, frowning at them. 'The rest of us a little less so. But that still doesn't answer Miss Mistry's question. What are you children doing here?'

'They just wanted to show me around before my first day,' you say.

Your new classmates all shoot you grateful glances.

'As admirable as that is, you shouldn't be here without the teachers,' Mrs Creecher tells them all.

Then her nose begins to twitch.

Uh-oh! you think.

'Does anyone smell . . . trifle?' she asks, scratching her head in puzzlement.

'NO!' shouts EVERYONE, AS LOUD AS THEY CAN!

'I was only asking!' grumbled Mrs Creecher.

'Probably just the leftover smell from school dinners,' you suggest.

'Yes, that will be it,' agrees Mrs Creecher. 'Well, you all run along home. I need to be heading back myself. I'm going to take a long bath.' She strides over to the top of the stairs. 'I'll see you all tomorr—OH!'

SHRIEK!

Mrs Creecher vanishes. Minnie facepalms. Miss Mistry runs to the stop of the stairs.

'Who left a slip and slide on the stairs?' she asks severely.

Nobody thinks they'll get detention on their first day at a new school.

And nobody even dreams the whole school will get detention!

Turns out Pie Face had made his giant pie, after all. While the other students had frantically tidied the school, he figured they'd need a snack after all their hard work. But with no one there to help him choose a flavour, he'd decided to bake not one, but ALL of his favourite flavours – in one pie! His mushroom, apple, cheese, broccoli, pumpkin, fish, maple and pecan pie is served as a detention snack.

201

But that's what it's like at Bash Street
School. It's like other schools, only funnier!
You think you're going to like it. A LOT!

THE END

DRAW YOURSELF AS A
BASH STREET KID!

Start with a rough circle with a curved cross in it. No need to be tidy – this is just a guide!

The centre of the cross points in the direction your drawing is facing.

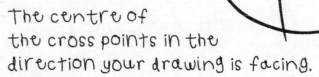

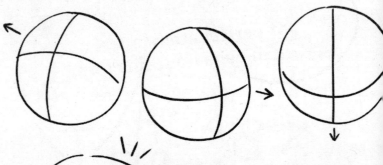

This will help you line up all the bits of face, so you don't wind up with an ear up your nose!

Add a chin to get your head shape right. Don't worry about it being EXACTLY the same as in real life - it's always fun to exaggerate it!

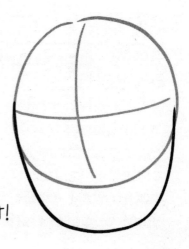

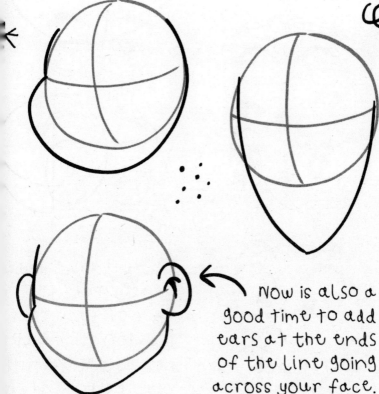

Now is also a good time to add ears at the ends of the line going across your face.

Eyes and eyebrows are super expressive and can show off your personality!

What mood are your eyes in today?

TOP TIP! You don't need to draw a full circle for each eye. Circles are hard!

You can pretty much draw any shape to make a nose.
Which nose will you pick? LOL!

The top of the nose should go in the middle, below the cross.

Like eyes, mouths are very

EXPRESSIVE!!

Try pulling funny faces in the mirror to see which one you like best!

Hair can be tricky to get right!
You can style it in stages to make
it easier to draw.

Start with a general
blobby shape...

Then draw the
details and
extra wispy bits
on top.

Flick through the book
at all the different
hairstyles for inso if
you like!

Remember to add all the accessories
and extras that make you, YOU!

HATS!

GLASSES!

HEADPHONES!

FRECKLES!

HERE'S A BLANK PAGE TO DRAW
YOURSELF ON! (and not because we
had a page left-over and ran
out of time — honest!)

TOP of the CLASS!

About the Authors

Craig Graham and Mike Stirling were both born in Kirkcaldy, Fife, in the same vintage year when Dennis first became the cover star of Beano. Ever since, they've been training to become the Brains Behind Beano Books (which is mostly making cool stuff for kids from words and funny pictures). They've both been Beano Editors, but now Craig is Editorial Director and Mike is Creative Director (ooh, fancy!) at Beano Studios. In the evenings they work with their genius Ed, Steph, at the Beanotown Boomix factory, experimenting and inventing new and exciting ways to let more kids than ever before discover how much fun reading can be! It's the ultimate Beano mission!

Craig lives in Fife with his wife Laura and amazing kids, Daisy and Jude. He studied English so this book is smarter than it looks (just like him). Craig is partially sighted, so he bumps into things quite a lot. He couldn't be happier, although fewer bruises would be a bonus.

Mike is an International Ambassador for Dundee (where Beano started!) and he lives in Carnoustie, famous for its legendary golf course. Mike has only ever played crazy golf. At home, Mike and his wife Sam relax by untangling the hair of their adorable kids, Jessie and Elliott.

PREVIOUSLY IN BEANOTOWN...

DON'T MISS DENNIS AND MINNIE'S FUNNIEST ADVENTURES!